Tales from the
CANYONS of
the DAMNED

PRESENTED BY USA TODAY BESTSELLING AUTHOR
DANIEL ARTHUR SMITH

Tales from the Canyons of the Damned 34

First Edition

Special thanks to editor Jessica West

ISBN: 978-1-946777-90-4

Cover By Daniel Arthur Smith

Horror Fiction from Holt Smith ltd
Agroland
Tower
Attack of the Kung Fu Mummies

For Susan, Tristan, & Oliver, as all things are.

Exclusionary Symbiosis
Nathan M. Beauchamp

DASHER'S RADIAL ENERGY MATRIX roasted well over a thousand bugs a second, and that suited Jaxson just fine. He'd grown to like the sizzle of the bugs frying. It was just about the only thing he took any joy in since arriving at Delta Centauri. Cruising at ninety knots, the matrix burned an estimated 67,000 bugs a minute, almost four million an hour. A rain of guts that reminded him of his grandma's lemon meringue pie filling fell over the still living bugs churned beneath *Dasher's* wake.

A glaze of orange light shrouded *Dasher's* cockpit, giving the endless oncoming swarm of insects a distinctive amber glow. Jaxson spat a stream of tobacco against the inside of the matrix—the real stuff, not the fake shit hawked at Kniles Exploratory. It slid down the interior wall and dribbled onto stained decking. Twenty-thousand volts on the outside, safe as kittens on the inside. Another bit of wizardry cooked up by the eggheads back at Earth. He sometimes wondered how they'd they tested the energy matrix. Go-fast boats racing across a Louisiana Bayou, shredding dragon flies and thumb-sized mosquitos? Because despite the fancy name, the matrix wasn't much more than a super pricey bug zapper.

And there were a shit ton of bugs to zap on Delta. Nothing but bugs, other than the three-story tall, fibrous plants reminiscent of broccoli. The bugs ate the plants in the warm months, popped out trillions of new young, died, and fertilized the decimated plants for the next growing season. The scientists called it "the most extreme form of exclusionary symbiosis ever discovered." Bugs. Plants. Life. Death. The scientists figured it had all been going on for over a hundred million years, other forms of life on Delta expunged.

It pissed Jaxson off that the first life aside from bacteria that humans had discovered on one of the half-dozen Earth-like planets reached by humans was nothing more than worthless bugs. He'd only signed up for Delta when he'd heard there'd be bugs to kill. He'd grown up watching the same old classic movies as other grunts: the fifteen-part *Starship Troopers* series; *Aliens*—the original movies and the remakes; the new-wave B-movies like *Sector Nineteen*. Fighting bugs seemed like the right mix of glamor and danger something to tell girls about on furlough. He'd never imagined it would be about as exciting as driving an old taxi through a bug hurricane.

The bugs had no end, and despite the muted savage pleasure he took in exterminating them, he could run supplies from the landing site at Kniles out to Proxima research station for two lifetimes and not make a dent in the alien population. *Aliens*. What a joke that had turned out to be.

They'd given up on trying to send orbitals directly to Proxima. Constantly shifting magnetic fields played chaos with nav systems, and extreme winds made landings hazardous. After a second orbital ended up nose-first in Delta's loamy soil, the higherups made the call to run skiffs like *Dasher* from Kniles to Proxima and back. It might have been an interesting job if it required actual piloting. But no—*Dasher* followed beacons a meter deep in the ground, the AI-assist running the course without any intervention on Jaxson's part. He was along for the ride as a maintenance tech, and usually spent the three-hour journey watching vids on his handscreen, eating, or staring out into the whirl of bugs, wishing he was on a torch ship back to Earth.

Nav control let out an all-too-cheerful chime. Another beacon crossed. Twenty minutes to Proxima. Jaxson stood and stretched his back. He hoped they'd be serving the spaghetti dinner at Proxima mess. The scientists had good food, he'd give them that. What the hell they were researching at Proxima? Well that was a big goddamned secret, way above his paygrade. Not that he didn't get curious. The same bugs and plants stretched from one end to the other of Delta's single continent. What was different at Proxima?

Another chime. Another beacon crossed. One hundred and eighty in total, he counted them subconsciously on each journey. Only nineteen more to go.

Another chime.

Then a sound Jaxson had never heard before. A sizzling *pop*, almost like a coil gun bolt lancing out to strike a target. But the sound came from *inside* the skiff. Another sizzling pop, and the matrix fell away, exposing the hull to a crush of insects. Jaxson leapt to his feet.

Then his feet left the deck and he was suspended for a half-second, just long enough to know that what came next was going to hurt like hell.

The deck slammed into his chest and he bounced.

The skiff tilted sideways.

Jaxson managed a bloody mouthed, "Shit," before the front windbreak caved and bugs roiled through the bent opening. He had the presence of mind to grab a wall stantion before the skiff hit ground for the final time. His arm damn near ripped free of his shoulder when it did.

Shaking with adrenaline, his skiff grounded, Jaxson took a few painful breaths of the remaining oxygen before the rest vented out into Delta's hydrogen-helium air. He forced his battered body toward the emergency locker.

Bugs crawled over the outside of the locker.

Pink, pearlescent, winged, thumb-sized—something like a wasp but without stingers. Three body sections like an insect, eight legs like an arachnid. Jaxson was too shook up to care about the bugs picking their way up his uniform pants or the bugs exploring the blood oozing out of a deep gash in his dislocated left arm. *Training. Follow your training.* He got out the mask, breathing apparatus, exo assist module. *Mask first, activate the chest pack, three controlled breaths…* Cool air laced with pain killers filled his lungs. *Activate neuro controls to link to the exo…*

Serpentine bands found his ankles, quads, waist, and the exo blossomed around his body, supporting his weight with biopneumatics and synthetic muscle fiber. The meds had enough kick to make the rollout process both surreal and euphoric. He was like a bug himself now, body shrouded and strengthened by the exosuit. Maybe it was just the drugs, but for the first time in months, Jaxson felt a small burst of happiness.

Emergency procedures complete, Jaxson looked around the skiff, trying to locate the source of the critical failure. A bit of oily smoke lingered in the cabin and streaks of electrical burn marred the nearest control board. Massive electrical blowout, maybe from the capacitors that kept the matrix humming. Once the matrix dropped, insects had filled the jets and destroyed them. Far more than he could fix. He hoped the AI-assist had notified Kniles of the crash before losing power. If it had, all he needed to do was wait for help to arrive.

Thousands—tens of thousands—of bugs had made it inside the cabin. They clung to every surface, crawled over the exosuit, fluttered against his face mask. How he'd managed to get that on without trapping bugs inside he'd never understand, but he was damned grateful that at least his face was free of bugs.

The dull thrum of distant pain played in harmony with his elevated heartrate. Seconds became minutes. No com, no sat link, and magnetic fields too strong to pierce with his in-suit radio. What if the colossal failure had wiped the AI-assist before it could message Kniles? What if nobody knew what had happened? They'd figure it out, eventually, when *Dasher* didn't make her arrival time at Proxima. But how long would that take? Longer than his oxygen supply?

Be calm. You've got ten hours' worth. Help is on the way.

But what if it wasn't?

He checked the supply gauge on his oxygen. The analog dial seemed to be moving faster than it should. He'd already dropped below the eight-hour mark. How was that possible? Was he leaking air?

He checked the supply, the line, the mask. Found no fault.

But the dial was working its way downward, and fast.

The skiff was *filling* with bugs. Bugs up to his ankles. Bugs on top of bugs. What if they stuffed the skiff to the brim? What if so many bugs piled inside he couldn't get back out?

Jaxson didn't make the decision to exit the skiff so much as leaving became an absolute necessity, like when he'd emptied his guts in the middle of mess after coming down with some sort of super bug. *Super bug.* The words rattled inside his hollowed-out skull. Ideas were getting damned blurry. Was that from the meds?

Outside, Delta's blue light gave the bugs a much different appearance, their milky bodies a burnished sapphire as they dove and skittered beneath the harsh shadows cast by the broccoli towers. Jackson had never seen them like this, nothing but a face plate between his eyeballs and them. Their slow and rhythmic movement was so different from the pelting deluge caused by the skiff's speed. They had a stately air to them. Unhurried yet purposeful.

The oxygen dial reached seven and a half hours, though only a minute or two had passed. Jaxson did some quick mental math. He'd need to hurry to reach Proxima before he exhausted his air supply. Assuming the leak wasn't getting worse. If it came down to that, he'd take off the mask and let the local air knock him unconscious. A better way to go than sucking at scraps of oxygen. Maybe the bugs would eat his body. That'd be fair, considering how many of the bastards he'd killed in his short time on Delta.

Delta's home star had started to sink in the southern sky, further lengthening the broccoli tower shadows. Jaxson trudged over loose soil, leaving giant, exosuit boot prints behind. A great accompaniment of bugs seemed to follow at each side, whirling and darting, some taking a brief rest on his exosuited body. He thought of flicking them free, but decided it wasn't worth the effort. The bugs couldn't do him any real harm.

Meters beneath his feet, interconnected hives linked by countless passageways ran. Linked in the same way as the broccoli towers' root systems intertwined, an even larger biomass than Earth's aspen groves. He'd seen images of cross-sections of the hives. The bugs had no queens like earth's ants or bees. Every bug could lay eggs, and every bug could fertilize them.

With night coming on fast, the wind picked up, whipping past his helmeted ears at thirty knots. No way could he make much forward progress without the exosuit. He pushed on into the stream, visor HUD laying down a silver pathway over the soil. It took him eight minutes to reach the next beacon, and by that time, his oxygen supply was down to six hours.

He wouldn't make it to Proxima before he ran out.

Like hell I won't.

Through the neuro connect, he boosted power to the exo muscle fibers and began to run, taking giant leaps forward in Delta's seventy-three percent of Earth's gravity. Each leap rattled his ribcage and sent shudders of pain down his spine, pain too strong for the meds to dull. He might beat his body to a pulp in the process, but he was going to make it to *Proxima.*

On his next forward leap, the rubberized foot pads of the exo slammed through Delta's crust, miring him up to his shins in soil. Momentum carried him forward headfirst, sprawled out, wind knocked from his chest. It took many painful seconds to regain his air. He pushed upright, trying to breathe steadily, trying to save as much oxygen as he could—

A bug hovered directly in front of his faceplate. He blinked, thinking the fall had somehow affected his vision. Blinked again. The bug remained, wings rotating like copter blades, its eyeless face inline with his own. Twenty times larger than it should be, its bulbous abdomen tipped by a distinctive, silver-blue stinger.

Jaxson lashed out at the bug with a closed fist.

Too late.

The stinger tip punctured the exo like a knifepoint through cellophane. Agony. Blinding, maddening agony, too intense to allow a scream, every muscle taught as though hit with a stun baton. Agony that faded, dulled, became a warm current flowing through his veins. He slumped to his knees, the giant bug's hooked feet clinging to the exosuit. The pain dissipated, replaced by profound calm. He let himself fall onto his back, still face-to-eyeless face with the bug. In a half-second, he relived the dozens of journeys he'd made from Kniles to Proxima, the tens-of-billions of bugs he'd destroyed. He regretted that so much. So, so much. He saw how wrong he had been, how wrong fleet command had been for coming to *Delta* in the first place.

Not Delta. No, this place had another name. A much more ancient name that could only be spoken with a series of sub-audible clicks and the whirl of wings...

You will help us.

He almost laughed with joy.

He *would* help. He would undo what had been done.

Dimly, as if from the vantage point of another set of eyes, he saw the oxygen meter pass its halfway point. It didn't concern him. Didn't concern *us*.

Us. This time the laugh broke free, gurgling upward out of his swollen stomach. Bloody saliva streaked his lips and chin. *Us.* Filled to overflowing with so many, many,

many. A gift for the hot bodies at Proxima. He saw—not with eyes but with the shadowy shapes produced by sound waves—the shuffling, pasty, malformed bodies of the scientist descending cold vertical shafts into the under-deep. Down to where the third participant in the symbiosis of life and death, of eating and reproducing, dwelled in secret darkness. Disturbed, removed, and cut open. Hurt and more hurt caused by the hot bodies, each protected by sunhot burn walls that not even the strongest of them could penetrate.

Rage burned within.

Rage, and a need to set things right.

Us.

How could rage and joy be so intimately intertwined?

Buoyed by a thousand-thousand kin, they flew through the mounting dark, onward to *Proxima.*

Ship of the Dead

Charles Barouch

PLANET-BOUND FOLK DON'T understand what it's like to mine asteroids. We don't get to take anything for granted, like air, water, or even a place to die. Eighty percent women up here. Seventy percent black. That makes The Belt one of the few places where I'm in the majority. I don't do the mining myself. That's another thing the grounders don't think about: for the mines to work, someone has to be up here to patch up ships, cook food, and do other necessary things. Me, I haul bodies to where the sun can pull them in and burn them proper. Just one of the curve balls life threw me.

Yesterday was a hard one. Mine on *2008 AZ* collapsed. Lost my best friend and a lot of drinking buddies. Worse is, I had to mourn them and haul them. Hard to pretend all that "in a better place" crap when you watch them flame out.

"Brenna!" Harley screamed through the comm.

"I hear you same, shout or not," I said. "What fresh hell you got for me, Harley Baer?"

"We have a complaint," he said.

A complaint. Now that was a new one on me. My fares don't have anything left to say by the time I get them. I waited instead of answering, mostly 'cause I knew it would annoy him. That man thought he was my boss. He should remember that I pay him, not the other way around.

"Some damn per-son-age of the grounders thinks you did something wrong," Harley said.

I asked him for details and got a lot of nothing for my troubles. That meant I couldn't handle it from the deck of the *Yawn* like I wanted to. I'd have to come back to base and check the logs. I don't know why I keep him. He's lazy. He don't ask good questions. He don't keep good notes. I have to push him to do each little thing. 'Course, that's why he has the time to work for me. Everyone had already shut the door on old Harley Baer.

I set the autopilot for base and went in for a nap. I figured I could get in three or four hours given the normal jam at the dock. Turned out to be closer to five.

"*Yawn*, you are clear for Northside Slips, proceed to berth four," said the Traffic Control Warden.

It was archaic and stupid. The ship took the instructions and did everything itself. They didn't need to go announcing it. Still, the call was my wake-up signal. Ten minutes to make myself presentable. I showered recent enough, so I used the time to fix an energy drink, sort my hair, and check my credit balance. If I was on base, I might as well resupply and hit a few relaxations.

I stepped off once we were clear. Northside had good seams, so I didn't need a suit to leave the ship. Southside had that accident back a year or so...lost six folks. I keep track of that sort of stuff; of how many died. Occupational habit. Worst luck for others is my good luck. I hate this job.

My office was just two corridors in from Northside. The warden put me in near a berth, so it was a quick walk. Harley, to my shock, was actually doing his job when I walked in. He had a customer sitting with him and he'd even remembered to beam her a rate sheet. I saw my logo on the flimsy in her hand. Miracles do happen.

"Harley," I said in my least irritated voice, "when you're done helping that nice lady, how about you and I talk about that call from Earth."

My tone didn't fool him any. He knew I only came back early 'cause he was being an ijit. The lady looked up and I realizes she wasn't one of us. This was a grounder, up here in my crappy little office. She wasn't a new client. She was the problem I came to figure out.

"I'm Allison Washington," she said. "You must be Brenna Childs."

"I must," I said, attempting a joke.

It didn't land. She looked at me like I was stupid. I started to reach for my hair—a nervous habit—but I stopped myself from giving in to the urge. She just kept staring. It was like some sort of a contest. I broke first.

"What can I do for you?" I finally said.

"I'm from Beyonder Services. We run the part of the government which licenses your business," Ms. Washington said.

She showed me her flimsy, which now displayed her credentials instead of my rate sheet. I pulled mine out of my pocket and unrolled it. She made a flicking gesture and her details beamed over. I made a point of looking, 'cause you should. I didn't care what it said. People like me end up dancing for people like her all the time. The particulars didn't matter. Not this time, not ever.

"So, what'd I do wrong? Not common for ground...er, planet-bound folk to visit," I said.

"Oh, no, nothing like that," Ms. Washington said. "We are here to see about expanding your charter."

"My business only gets bigger if people die," I said. "Are you in the business of killing folks?"

"I'm explaining myself badly," Ms. Washington said. "We expect that emigration from Earth to the Beyond will be rising. Since there are only two of you in your...unique line of business..."

"Let me guess," I said. "You mean me and Pegger Smith. And you can't seem to get Pegger's attention? And now I have to explain to you what I've already told twenty others just like you. Pegger was in the business. She had a nice little ship called the *Dawn Fire*. When she started getting on in years, she took me on. I was between mines, 'cause the one I was working had played out. We were partners for five years before old Pegger ended up riding in the back, if you take my meaning. I always called the *Dawn Fire* the *Yawn Fryer* because it bugged her. When she died, I made the name official."

"We'll have to update our records," Ms. Washington said.

"That's what the last twenty said," I told her.

She tried to start talking again, so I faked a yawn and asked nicely if we could do this after I'd had a chance to catch up my paperwork and my rest. She bought it and we agreed to meet for dinner.

Southside Inner had a nice Italian place. Never been on Earth, so I can't speak to how authentic it is, but I like it. Odds are, Washington's paying, so I expect to like it extra this time.

As soon as the door closed behind her, I lit into Harley. He'd called it a complaint when it wasn't. He didn't tell me it was 'in person' instead of just a 'net thing. He sure as hell didn't tell me she was from Earth when I walked in. And she was government on top of that. If I wasn't the only ijit who could meet her need, that coulda been important.

"Brenna," Harley said when I finally had to pause for breath.

"Yes?" I asked.

"Nothing. You are every ways right," he said.

I knew this act. He sounded contrite. He put up the puppy dog eyes. It always worked on Pegger. Difference was, I wasn't his cousin. She had to put up with him. I ran the list of people who might replace him through my head. Four of them were in yesterday's haul. It looked like I had to put up with him, too. Thing is, none of those four would have taken the job. They liked the life. Me, I was happy to get halfway out. Doing this meant I kept out of the mines but stayed in The Belt. It was a fair deal. Still hate it, though.

"One more screw up, Harley Baer," I threatened, "and we'll see if a live one burns any slower than the dead."

I'd just had my nap, so I used the whole of the stall time to catch up on paperwork. Don't know why we still call it that. I haven't seen anything but a flimsy for three years now. Last I was at the Doc, and she had a diploma. I thought it was paper but she said something about being animal skin. I don't see much of that here either, 'less you count human animals.

Fifteen death certs were waiting on my finish up. Harley could do every part but seal them, but somehow everything was left for me. If I didn't have a legal requirement on having this office, I'd boot his butt back to Earth with one swift kick. That man hit every nerve by the end of any given month.

I did the certs, I paid the bills—also his job—and finished up by ordering some MRE for the Yawn. I get lazy about cooking by the end of a tour and skipping meals can be fatal. Keeping alive takes energy.

My momma used to tell me and my sister Crystal that sharp was the word you needed most in space. Avoid sharp objects. Look sharp. Dress sharp. Keep a sharp tongue so you don't get taken. She used to joke that my sister was named Crystal to remind her to be sharp. Me? I never needed a reminder.

I was prompt to the restaurant, but the government lady wasn't. When you know how much air costs, you resent anyone who makes you waste it. Sitting here, cooling my heels, was just that: waste. When she showed up, she was, as my momma used to say, space blue. It's how grounders sometimes get when they breathe our air for too long. She wasn't acclimating well. For some reason, that made me happy.

I could have gotten up and helped her to the table. I could have told her that every restaurant and store was equipped with gentle-breathers. Instead, I sat and watched her space blues take her lungs for a ride. Whatever we ordered tonight, odds are, I was the only one eating.

"So, you want to up the death rate," I said conversationally.

Washington fumbled a pill case out of her pocket and washed it down with a sip of water. It seemed to work near instant, but that might just be the anticipation lending her strength. When the pill and that sip hit her stomach, I saw it on her face. She kept it together and finally got to talking.

"Burse Co. is expanding and that means less space for people. We in the government have been suing them to give back some of the land, but they are just too big to oppose. We expect perhaps ten percent of the remaining Earth population will be looking at The Belt for living space."

"Ten percent? What's that leave?" I asked. "Sounds to me like you have just enough land to hold the Burse employees and the government ones."

"Closer to the truth than most people will admit," she said.

I'd rather not have been right.

"Fact is, in ten years, there'll be more people in the Beyond than on Earth," she added.

Her conversation was too frank. Things must be worse than I thought if she was admitting this much. 'Course, The Belt can't support that many. Even if most of them go to the Moon and Mars, we're damn close to limits as-is. I didn't say that, though. I wasn't here to school this grounder. I was here to eat some free Italian food and let her talk.

"What do you want me to do?" I asked.

"We want you to spin up two more ships," she said.

I nearly spit out the sip of water I just took. The waitress came by, finally, and I waved her off. I had to hear this proper. How was I going to spin up anything? No money and no crew. Keeping Harley was a luxury. What did she think I made in a month of doing this?

"We'll pay for everything," Ms. Washington said, guessing my train of thought.

That pill must have tilted her brains. Government never gave me anything. They're in the business of taking.

"When you say pay, and I mean this kindly, do you know what spinning up a ship costs?" I asked it as calmly as I could.

"Three million credits for each ship," she said like she was discussing the price of the side dishes, "A quarter more for the refit to meet government regulations. Eight thousand credits to train each captain in final protocols...Do I need to go on?"

"And you're just gonna Fargo me six and a half mil?" I tried to match her casual tone.

"Nine million, even," Ms. Washington said. "Your current ship deserves an overhaul. We might go a little higher if you put in a grant request for a better office."

The waitress came back. I wanted to wave her off, but I didn't have the spare attention to do that. Ms. Washington ordered the fire-roast vegetable appetizer. I guess that pill really did fix her space blues. I was having my own sort of blues. I only owned the *Yawn* because Pegger willed it to me. I'd never earn the three million to buy a stock ship, much less the other costs. Hell, my ship was sixteen years old when I got it, and I couldn't have bought it used, even if you stacked my income for the last five years against it. Damn.

"I'll have papers for you tomorrow," Ms. Washington said as she picked up her water glass.

I just looked at her. She said numbers that big like they bored her. I pointed at something on the menu as the waitress tapped her foot. My mouth still wasn't working. I grabbed up my water because drinking it gave me something to do while I gathered my wits. Be sharp, momma said.

"I'll look over the papers," I said.

When the appetizer arrived, Ms. Washington told the waitress to bill the meal to her account. She finished off one bite of carrot and left. I sat alone. I ate the vegetables while I waited for whatever I'd ordered. When the waitress returned, I was happy to see a steak. Guess that was what I pointed at. 'Case you don't know, free steak tastes extra good. I ordered another. After that, I ordered dessert to go.

I took my bag of zeppole and went back to the ship. I don't maintain apartments on base. That's a cost I don't need to pay. Sleep was hard that night. I had two helpings of steak in my belly and nine million credits dancing in my head. The morning started with a shower and a careful pass through my closet. I needed to look extra sharp.

Ms. Washington was there half an hour after I opened. She beamed me the contracts. I started reading.

"Now, did you think you could slip this past me because I'm home-schooled? Or do you just think that all Beyonders are gullible?" I asked it with venom in my voice.

"We don't slip anything past anyone," Ms. Washington said. "We're the government."

I nearly choked on that.

"Last night, you didn't say anything about this being a loan," I accused. "I can't pay back nine million. Even without interest. And you have that set to ten percent. I thought ten percent interest was illegal."

"Skip to the second document. You can finish the first one later," she said.

I skipped. The second document assigned the debt to Burse Co. To my shock, that one was already counter-signed. Burse was picking up the tab.

"How'd you get them to do it?" I asked.

"Part of how they've been stalling our lawsuit," Ms. Washington said. "They keep donating money to soften the impact of their actions."

"So, I borrow from the government, and Burse gets the payment book?" I asked.

"Take your time reading," Ms. Washington said.

I took my time. There were six contracts in all. They all referenced each other. I was jumping from page to page and document to document. It took me a long time to be sure I didn't miss anything. I found three paragraphs which I'd overlooked on the first pass. I read every bit. Then I read it again. It was a sadistic piece of work. Everything had a rule-set explaining how I was allowed to spend it. Every rule-set had a penalty condition. It'd be like blind-driving in a minefield to get everything done.

Together, the contracts made my head spin but I'm pretty smart so I got through it. When I was done, there were two things which were very clear. No regular person could ever-ever-ever get away the crap in this set of contracts. The other thing was that I had to say yes. With this much free money, they'd get someone to say yes if I didn't.

I sighed and I signed. Ms. Washington gave me a reassuring smile. I didn't feel right about any of this. I remembered my manners and walked her to the docks. The happier she looked, the more my stomach twisted.

Because it was the government, everything took time. From the day I signed, the life I was satisfied with before the contracts, now it felt like a cheap imitation. I was living in the between; still poor but no longer handling it. It made me less sharp. I nearly final-banged the ship twice that first week. Miners mean asteroids. Asteroids mean *pay attention when you fly*.

Eventually, I settled back into my old ways. I wasn't raised to spend money that hadn't arrived. Mama's wisdom was still protecting me. When the transfer finally went through, I was slow to proceed. How do you make peace with spending that much money?

Ms. Washington, who had been unreachable for the last six months, started calling me. She wanted progress reports. I'd agreed to that, so I had to make some progress to report. Harley turned out to be pretty good at evaluating mechanics. I guess everyone has something they can do. We found a decent ship—made by Burse, no surprise—and a local shop to do the refits. Bigger shops on the Moon and Mars, but I like spending local.

The plan was pretty simple. Build one new ship. I'd captain it while *Yawn* got fixed up. Then, at the tail end, buy the other. Finding captains, that was another matter.

It wasn't the long alone times. Most people up here were okay with that. Trouble was, the ones who could navigate—you can't just trust the automatics—already had work. I didn't just want to out-pay their current jobs. I wanted ships to pay for themselves—for the day-to-day costs at least. I even gave Harley a tryout. He final-banged eight times on the simulator, so I didn't let him near the real controls. Deadlines where looming. I needed a break.

Worst luck for others is my good luck. Three mines tapped out at once. That took me from no applicants to plenty. I snatched up the best two, an ore hauler named Smitty and a miner named Doves. They still needed training, but I had barely enough time to get everything done.

Last Mosey had been in service for two months. *Yawn Fryer* was out of repairs. I'd have the third ship in the next week or two. Still needed a name for it. Things were coming together.

Harley found a loophole. Seems that a pilot could skip the training if they could beat the tests without. I took them on *Yawn* and trained the hell out of them for ten days. I hated sharing space on my ship, but I did what needed doing. They passed on the first try. I teamed them up on *Last Mosey* until we had the last ship.

The big day finally arrived. Our third ship was ready. I was back on Northside this time 'cause I'd called *Last Mosey* in so Smitty and Doves could celebrate with me. The predicted influx of grounders had started last month and they were accident prone up here. I'd been very busy. We'd all been busy. I hate when business is good.

With the third ship was arriving, I thought it was going to be a good day. It wasn't. We took in a big lunch while we waited for the *Pegger's Dream* to be delivered. We, my captains and me, were in shock when we walked over to Northside berth sixteen to see our third ship.

She didn't have her name on her nose. Instead, it had a Burse logo and a registration number. Not the logo it had when it came from the factory – 'cause this was a stock Burse ship originally—this one said 'Burse Final Solutions.' A man stepped off the ship. He wasn't from the repair team I hired to refit it. This one had on a grounder business suit. I knew enough to tell he was just a messenger. The grounder made that flicking gesture which beamed something to my flimsy. I took it out of my pocket to look.

*

Ms. Childs,

As a result of the unfavorable conclusion of the government's most recent lawsuit against us, your funding arrangement with Burse

Co. has been terminated. Your ships will be taken as collateral until you complete all payments. The current bill, with interest, will be sent under separate cover. In consideration of your situation, Burse Co. is willing to offer you employment in our new venture, Burse Final Solutions. Upon reviewing your most recent flight license renewal, we have determined that you do not meet our standards for pilots. Accordingly, we will make an office job available. The details of that offer will also arrive under separate cover.

To further ease your mind, we intend to offer Winny Smith and Jackie Doves positions as well. We do not, unfortunately, have a position for Harley Baer at this time.

We thank you for doing business with us and look forward to working with you in the future.

- *Allison Washington, Director of New Business, Burse Co.*

Last Visit to the Park

Terry R. Hill

NINETEEN THOUSAND, FOUR HUNDRED and ninety-six days. Give or take a day or two. Maybe a week. At this point, what difference does it make? That's when everything changed, and sure-as-hell not for the better.

His old bones pushed against his thinning muscles as the cold plastic seat of the subway lurched with every bump of the rails. The car was empty; the only sign of life was a reflection in the window across from him, of an old man sitting and eating a bag of cashews. He wore a coral-colored, droopy fisherman's hat and an unbuttoned, sea blue shirt over a purple t-shirt, with blue and white pinstriped shorts. His body bent as if the world had hung on him for generations. He had been young and strong once, but it was hard to believe those days had blown away so quickly like yesterday's afternoon storm.

Setting the bag of nuts down, he looked to the ring on his left hand; smoothed gold by years of wear, and an insignia surrounded by a black field. That symbol meant something once ago. Something special. Something that people died for. In the end, it meant a lifetime of loneliness, the vacuum within growing stronger while he remained surrounded by millions of strangers; waiting for decades for a familiar face was too much to bear any longer. Tonight, he would do what the Universe was too cowardly to commit; tonight, he would let the cold freeze solid what was left of his heart.

The glass window pane was cold as he slowly drew on the inside frost, watching it melt around his finger. It was the morning evidence he was still alive and not some postmortem dream. This morning, he'd watched the day break as the sun rose far beyond the overcast sky. The muted light was the deciding measure. He had struggled with the decision for quite some time, but the cold, grey morning was the final unbearable metaphor. The memory of his first visit to an old-folks home was still uncomfortably vivid. It was foreign. Everyone was so old, sick, and obnoxiously close to death. The place reeked of lineament, bleach, and shit. Yep, that's exactly how his apartment smelled now. How soon it had happened.

For his entire life, he had looked up at the glinting night sky and felt a longing to explore out in the black expanse of space. Wanderlust is for the young and reckless, but for the last half of his life, it had only grown. A yearning. A quickening of the heart. A calling to go to a home somewhere amid the stars, so strong he would have willingly jumped on any alien ship that stopped by Earth with the promise to go someplace else. Somewhere far beyond his current reach…somewhere he would never see. He would live out the rest of his life and die on this little water-covered rock in the backwoods of the galaxy.

In the last few years, the excitement and longing had been replaced with pain and discomfort from just about every part of his body, plus a few not readily identified. Another new pain that wasn't there the day before, and a few which had been there longer than he could remember. Where had all the years gone? A young man who once started a new life in a faraway place was now an old man; not where he wanted to be. Yes, the decades had flown quickly, but paradoxically he was excruciatingly aware of every single day that had passed. Every doggedly slow minute. It is truly amazing how slow time passes when you're waiting for something very important to arrive but it never does.

Perhaps the years stretched out so long because there was no one with whom he could share them. Those who knew him over the years speculated as to why he never married. Shy, low self-esteem, gay, he'd heard all the gossip, none of it true of course and none of it remotely accurate. Gobsmacked. He'd always loved that phrase. Yes, gobsmacked would be a good way to describe their reaction if they ever knew his actual reason for never marrying.

Over the years, he had seen ships, rusted, requiring too much maintenance, spewing too much smoke, threatening to fail at any given moment, and decommissioned before they did. Now he understood how the ships must have felt. Gave all they had to the cause, working tirelessly for the reward of their contract with those they loyally served. However, the reality was they toiled away, day after day until they could go no more, then they were dismantled. And that was why he was going to Central Park today. It was his time. There were record low temperatures forecasted for tonight.

It was time to catch the train to Manhattan.

Normally, it was possible to ignore the typical sounds of the park when he sat and closed his eyes to think, but something niggled for attention in the corner of his mind. More and more of the days were spent this way, thinking about the plans for his life…and how things played out. It wasn't unusual for an old man to ruminate over lost days, but his story was different.

"We're civilized! There were measures put in place to keep this from occurring." Nothing like what happened to him had been heard of for a generation or more. But none the less, it did. Statistics, bad luck, or like the locals say, Karma.

Something poked at his attention again. What was it, a different sound other than the background squeaks of children in the distance or the roar of a plane overhead? Ah. Someone was standing nearby. Their presence weighed heavy like a stranger's shadow on a hot summer afternoon. Honestly, he didn't really care if they existed or not, but idle curiosity eventually won out.

Looking up through untamed eyebrows, he saw a young man standing next to him, dressed in an oversized hoodie, worn leather jacket, and a pair of jeans which appeared to have lost a fight with a wild animal. Of course, with fashion being what it was, it was impossible to tell if he was homeless or going out on the town. The young man's face told a story of harsh living and bad decisions. In the sixties, this young man would have been an outcast, a rebel, a bad seed; but today, he's the norm. The world's expectations and rules had flip-flopped during his life here. How civilization could march on with such reversals was beyond him.

"Hey, old man, anyone sitting here?" the young man asked, pointing at the park bench.

"What?" the old man grumbled. The cold January wind whipped around his head, biting his ears and nose as it tried to get inside his collar.

"I *said*, anyone sitting *here*?" said the young man with an accent and irritation.

The old man scanned the park around him, now empty but for him and this boy. Evidently, the rest of the city had enough sense to stay indoors today.

"Hmmph. Well, since the park's so crowded...if that'll let you die happy, be my guest."

The young man gave what sounded like a grunt of respect to a private joke and flopped down hard next to him. A bit too close, really. Maybe the boy wanted to take his money. Maybe he wanted to kill for the thrill. Maybe he was some perv. Either way, soon, it wouldn't matter much.

A strange smell pricked his nose. Between the dulling of age and living in New York City, one can grow to disregard certain smells, particularly the less pleasant. But this was something different, familiar. Like walking into an old building and the scents suddenly throw you back into your grandmother's home as a youngster, bringing back memories you'd forgotten about decades before. This boy, young man, his presence awakened memories of...

"Why are you sitting here?" the stranger asked.

"I do mind, the question. Who taught you conversational etiquette, a bouncer?" He glanced over to the young man without any discernable emotion. The dangerous ones were generally devoid of emotion. But for what he had planned today, anything violent would be a welcome end to it all.

"Fine...nothing."

"You know it's gonna be freezing soon."

"Thank you for minding my business, young man, but I need the fresh air. Now go away," he growled, immediately regretting engaging in another conversation with a stranger.

The young man nodded his head slightly and turned to look at him, the blankness gone and replaced with controlled irritation.

"You live around here?"

Damn, this boy won't catch a hint.

"Long enough to mind my own business. Look, I really don't want any company today. *Particularly* today." He didn't care any longer. Might as well piss the thug off and have him quickly and silently slide a thin blade between two ribs of his choice, take is ring, and move on.

Un-phased, the young man continued, "You have family close by? Where do they live?"

That did it, that was the last straw of nosiness!

"Look, son! I don't know what your game is—rob me, follow me home and steal my stuff later, try and steal my identity. Whatever your scam is, you should know that I have seen and heard it all before, and I am not your average senior citizen. So, keep your questions and your damn curiosity to yourself. Got it? Otherwise, I'm going to introduce you to a nice can of mace and a conversation with the police!" the old man said with a ferocity not matching his weathered exterior. The muscles of his face were in their practiced place of successful staring down both man and beast.

Slowly, the young man leaned in closer, his voice teetering on a decision as he placed a hand inside his jacket.

"Calm. Down."

The muscles in the old man began to relax a little with the inevitability of what this miscreant was about to deliver. He finally crossed the line. It wasn't how he'd planned it, but what was in his life?

"Sorry, just today I have something to do and having company…complicates things," he mumbled, backed down, and went back to picking through his bag of nuts, which was a better use of his time than telling his story to this damn whippersnapper. The young man looked away.

Pregnant moments passed.

The young man suddenly shifted, facing him again.

Why won't he leave?

"Look, old man, I…don't have much time. What's your story?"

Oh, he could tell him a few things to speed this all along. Maybe a second helping of minding his own damn business perhaps. Or some, 'Keep your perversion to yourself,' or perhaps some, 'Most people don't want to be your damn friend, particularly when they're trying to kill themselves!'

But…anything to get him to move on or do him the favor of quickening his plans along.

"Look, son, I'm not trying to be mean. Well okay, maybe I am, but at my age, I'm not going to apologize for that. It's just that no one has ever wanted to hear my story. I lived a life, but half of it no one can relate to, and I have something to do today."

"Proceed, but let's not prolong this," the stranger locked gaze with him, his cold eyes piercing deep inside of him. A shiver ran across his scalp.

"I mean what I said. No one, including you, can relate to most of my life. Let me speak slowly so it will sink into your young, thick head—you won't understand and think I'm crazy. It's a waste of my time," he snapped, returning to his nuts.

Think he was crazy? Maybe the reactions from the few he'd told his story to over the years were more accurate than he'd been willing to accept. Numerically speaking, if the same conclusion is reached multiple times via independent paths, it tends to represent reality. Maybe it's not a problem of the locals not being able to stretch their minds around his story. Maybe it was him who continued to stretch a story around a reality he didn't want to accept; a deluded narrative he continued to tell himself to cover for something missing in his life.

"Captain Radnower, sir," said the young man. A hint of a slight smirk threatened as his intense eyes continued to probe for something lost, then he growled, "Bet you didn't expect that, huh?"

"Captain? Were you with the Air Force or Navy?"

Radnower paused. "Yeah. I've seen my fair share of unbelievable stuff. Besides, who am I? Just an asshole on a park bench, like you. Try me, but let's not drag this out," he moved his hand from inside his jacket to rest on his leg.

A series of honks from a car in the distance passed as he considered the youth's offer. He gave Radnower a doubtful look. His gut told him to move and find some people for safety, but something else kept him on the bench.

What the hell, he'd entertain telling the story one more time. Morbid fascination of a man who had nothing to lose, won the roll of the dice to see how this would pan out. What did it matter now anyway? "Oh, all right, but I'll tell you again, you're wasting both our time."

Radnower nodded to continue, then slowly scanned the old man's jacket and pockets where his hands were buried.

"Fine, damnit. My name is Lieutenant Colonel Adis Nothan of the Lanthian Space Force, Cartography Wing," Adis began in an old man's 'arthritic sweet' time. "I was sent to this sector of the galaxy to survey and update the star maps."

"Lieutenant Colonels don't update maps," snapped Radnower.

"Yes, well, actually you're right, but," Adis paused, taken aback at the oddly germane remark, "I'd retired from a career in the Force, but I missed it so much and didn't really know how to live as a civilian. I re-enlisted with the cartography group so I could do a little traveling."

Radnower smirked and nodded slowly.

"They gave me a beautiful, one-seater recon scout ship - she was a beaut - and we sailed the winds that blew between the stars.

"My attention was drawn to this planet when I started picking up some very faint signals in the radio frequencies which were unusual for a star system like this. So, once I narrowed it to this unexpectedly habitable blue planet, I went into a circularized orbit to try and determine the source of the radio signals.

"The ship's sensor data had just started coming in indicating the emissions were coming from multiple points in the orbit and from the ground and the next thing I knew, there was a massive, blinding explosion off the left side of the ship and a second later–"

"What happened?"

"You want to hear the story or jump to the last page?" Adis barked.

Radnower remained silent and leaned back slightly.

Adis grumbled under his breath something about youth these days.

"Anyway, as I was saying, I passed out, and sometime later, I regained consciousness but that was more than I could say for my ship. She was mostly dead and in a slow tumble. I was able to reboot the emergency transponder, but couldn't functionally verify it because the ship was beginning to hit the upper parts of the atmosphere which increased the tumble rate of the ship, threatening to make me black out again—I was losing altitude fast. If I couldn't get some control back, I was going to burn up during re-entry. The landing part, I'd have to worry with that later.

Radnower made a sound under his breath while he extended one arm to rest on his knee, clenching it white knuckled. Tribal tattoos peaked out from under the jacket cuff, tickling some long-forgotten memory in Adis.

"Anyway, I couldn't establish power to the control thrusters, so I ripped out the power feed line from under the control panel and hot-wired it into the emergency computer power pack since it was the only system alive on the ship besides me. Things were happening fast, but a few sparks later, I got some intermittent control of the ship and pointed it in the right direction to survive the burn through the atmosphere.

"With the ship through the burning plasma, slowing, and relatively stable as it fell through the atmosphere, per my military training and working the most critical issue at a time, the next on the list was getting to the ground safely. There was nothing but water below me for as far as I could see to the horizon. Still, traveling around seven times the speed of sound, it wasn't long before I could see some land on the horizon. I used my attitude thrusters as best I could to continue slowing my descent with some hope of hitting it."

"Obviously, you landed safely," he said, slowly scanning the area.

"Long story short, I made it. Barely. In hindsight, I wonder if it'd have been better if I hadn't. Either way, I landed in what I later learned to be central Canada in the middle of nowhere. On my way down, I tried to send a distress signal home but I wasn't sure if it sent due to all the power I was diverting to the thrusters. Since no rescue's ever shown up, I guess that pretty much answers that question."

Radnower nodded slowly.

"I learned later that the explosion which disabled my ship was one of this planet's early orbital tests of nuclear weapons. As luck would have it, on July 9, 1962, the Starfish Prime test was launched from Johnston Island and detonated right next to my ship."

"That's before space program."

"I said I wasn't *from* this planet, boy! Anyway, the explosion caused a massive electro-magnetic pulse that my ship was not designed to withstand since we haven't used that technology on my planet for over a thousand years, so down I went. Hell, the explosion was so powerful it caused electrical damage in Hawaii, about 900 miles from the explosion."

Radnower's eyebrows raised slightly. "Surprising you survived."

"Good breeding, son. Plus a career as a military Space Force pilot.

"After a few days trekking through the damp alien forest, I finally made it to a town and tried to integrate into society as best I could. Fortunately, my image projection hardware had continued to function over the decades, which projects a 'human' form to the natives, allowing me to live and walk freely for the last half-century of this planet. However, in hindsight, I must have scared the hell out of that couple hiking in the forest that first day before I knew what the intelligent species—and I use that term loosely—looked like. Good ole Canadians, once they regained consciousnesses from the fright of seeing my natural form, they wished me good day and continued on." Adis let out a belly laugh which degraded into coughing spasms. Radnower stared with strained patience.

Adis regained his composure and continued. "Yeah, well, while the form projection technology makes me appear human while showing my representative age. And in the unlikely event you're in hostile territory for an extended period of time and aging is expected so as not to draw attention to yourself. Being away from my home world, I haven't had access to the needed microbiome to maintain my health and thus have aged significantly—more than normal. As it turns out, you humans live less than half as long as my people..." Adis' words trailed off as he got lost in memories from home.

After a few moments, Radnower cleared his throat.

"Oh yes, Scandinavian. I go by Eric Svenson now, since people thought my accent sounded Scandinavian. So, over the years, I made my way to New York. It's not the ideal place to be, but being around and watching you humans was better than living alone over the years. A few have tried to become friends with me, but while we could communicate just fine, as a species you're still very myopic. It's like trying to be friends with someone who only sees a foot or two of the ground around their feet and is oblivious to the universe around them. The conversation isn't exactly stimulating."

Radnower raised an eyebrow.

"But, you hold promise as a species, I suppose, if you can get your act together and make it through The Great Filter. Not many do, you know."

"Hmm. So, what did you do all of this time?" The young man showed some renewed interest.

Adis harrumphed. "I thought I'd better learn as much about the humans as I could before I was rescued because Central Command would want to know about this new species who were well on their way to space travel, at that time. Since your languages are fairly simple, I picked one up quickly and enrolled in one of the centers for higher learning. It was all very rudimentary and I might have even pointed them in the right direction in orbital mechanics and computational technology while studying as a graduate student...once the human space program got off the ground." Adis chuckled at the double meaning of the human words.

"Well, I guess I'm thinking like you now. Anyway, I went into engineering and eventually into the aerospace business sector. It had been a couple of decades since I crashed and decided I had best secure long-term provisions for myself in case a rescue party never arrived. Or at best, I could help sustain their rapid technology development with the hopes of being able to possibly gain the parts I needed to someday fix my ship.

"See, son, at that time, I was still in deep denial of the possibility of never being rescued. I couldn't come to terms with the fact I would always be marooned on an alien planet populated by a self-absorbed, troglodyte of a species. But because there was considerable momentum behind their space program, at least through the end of their twentieth century, I decided to help out a little here and there. In hallway conversations and low-level design meetings, I nudged them in the right direction in some orbital mathematics in the Mercury program. Later in the Apollo program, I might have helped them out with some of their early microcomputer hardware designs." Adis laughed, which spawned another series of coughs.

"I got them started out with some solar cell technology for their satellites and fuel pump technology for their Space Shuttle main engines. The way they were progressing, I hoped they might be well on their way to leaving your solar system by the time I grew too old. I would later learn of my folly on not anticipating your society losing interest in going into space, as well as the fact that I would age so much faster here. But I kept myself busy going from one company after another, mostly out of curiosity, but also it was better than dealing emotionally with the fact no one had come for me. No one. And they ... never would."

Radnower shifted on the bench impatiently.

"The years passed very quickly and my body aged surprisingly fast, but I guess it was normal for you humans. I retired from the workforce. I have to tell you, these years since then have been the hardest. Living with a body that is wearing out, always in pain, and malfunctioning in new and creative ways every day. This is not how we do it on my world. We extend the life of a body to its extreme then let them pass before they are trapped in a failed body..."

Adis drifted away in thought for a few moments. "See, I told you I was a crazy old man." He cocked an eyebrow to gauge the young man's reaction.

No sooner had their gazes connected, Radnower barked, "What's your personal ID?"

"What?"

"I said, what's your personal ID, soldier?"

As if driven by instinct, his ancient body moved automatically, struggling to stand. Why, he wasn't sure, but he saluted, "CD-4295-12 Cartography, sir!"

Radnower gave a broad smile filled with years of fistfights and bad dentistry. "Yeah, you're a serious crazy old man. Good story, though. Guess you earned getting this over fast." He fluidly rose to his feet, face to face with Adis.

For the first time ever, Adis flinched. A cold shiver raced down his spine. It was hard to know if the chill reached is feet first or his sinking heart. It had actually felt really good to tell his story to someone who seemed like they at least cared enough to listen without obvious judgement. So it *was* going to happen. The punk was just entertaining himself before he took out his mark for the day. Perfect day for it, no one around. This was just all fun and games for him. *No! I changed my mind. I want to wait just a little longer. Don't do this!* But no words came; the cold, dry air had stolen his voice.

Radnower pushed up the arm of his jacket and extended it slowly toward him. Adis' eyes widened slightly in question.

What? What did he want? Push an old man down? I don't understand.

The young man's hand froze midway between them.

Did he want to shake hands? Don't be an old fool, Adis! You probably fell asleep on the bench and this is all another damn dream…

Oh, what the hell? No way to stand against the strength of youth…

He reciprocated.

No sooner had they grasped, the young man's tattoos faintly glowed blue and a rush of energy burst forth, energizing Adis' old body, causing every hair to stand on end and his skin to crawl with the sensation of ten thousand ants. His body collapsed back onto the bench, void of any remaining strength.

Arrrgg! What...what's going on...this quickening...?

When the pain-fueled tunnel vision finally subsided, Adis held up his phone and stared wide-eyed at the reflection on the surface...where a *new* young man now sat.

"What have you done?"

Radnower smiled gently. "Lieutenant Colonel Nothan, congratulations, you've verified your identity." His voice and accent had shifted slightly.

"I'm from the Lanthian Space Force. I'm here to take you home. Sorry it took us so long. I hope you're feeling a little better now. Unfortunately, I have to report that there's been trouble which delayed things, and we're once again in need of your service."

Off-World Kick Murder Squad VII

Daniel Arthur Smith

This is the seventh episode of the serialized novel Off-World Kick Murder Squad. Earlier episodes can be read in the previous Canyons issues

COULDA, WOULDA, SHOULDA…If we hadn't taken on those lizard birds, if we'd launched the *Jentu* directly after she was prepped, hell if we'd have taken to sky a mere few minutes earlier—we would've been clear. But we didn't. And now it looked like we weren't going anywhere upward anytime soon, pinned down by a column of syndicate troopers and a half dozen artillery mechs—just one of which, by the way, could put enough hurt on our delta wing to ensure we'd never fly again.

Hodge was matter of fact about it. "That's a whole lot of ugly," he said.

While Bailer was typical in his surety. "They're not going to fire. Not as long as the Indici is on board."

"You think?" asked Anson.

"You'll see. They'll be calling, any second."

And on cue, a series of clicks purred from the com.

"You're right," said Anson. "We have a call coming in." He spun clear so I could see the incoming signal on the com screen.

"Okay," I said. "Let's see what they have to say."

Anson tapped the com button and the signal on the screen was replaced with the face of a smug little man in a pristine white uniform. On his lapel he wore the insignia of a lieutenant, but his eyes weren't blue like ours; he wasn't a Bureau officer or a syn, which didn't surprise me in the slightest. He was one of the Korean syndicate's private army and for their own reasons, they stuck to a certain low-level breed of human. I'd seen his like too many times before. This guy had never known a battle and was itching to blast at something other than the local spry lizards. Guys like him rarely waste time getting to brass tacks and when he opened his mouth, he proved me right. "Let's make this quick," he said. "Give us back what you took, we'll pay your crew over and above whatever your fee is, and you can be on your way."

I played it coy. "I don't think I know what you're talking about."

"Sure you do. You're bounty hunters, and I'm offering a higher bounty. High as you like. Name your price."

"You have us confused with someone other than ourselves. We're not bounty hunters. We're barely in the people moving business."

Putting him on edge was easy, he was already triggered. "Don't play semantics with me," he said. "Someone hired you to deliver your cargo for a fee. It's the same thing. Now I don't care what line you're in. Your business is your business. I'm even willing to overlook the mess you made at the station. I'm just saying I'll offer you more. It's better for you and your crew all the way around. I'll give you a minute to think it over."

The screen went blank.

"Hmm," said Bailer.

"Hmm, what?" asked Hodge.

Bailer leaned into the windscreen for a tighter inspection. "He's going to take us out as soon as we hand Cerulean over."

"Agreed," I said.

Hodge shrugged. "But what if he means it?"

"Means what?" I asked.

"Well," said Hodge, "he's right. More is more. Maybe he's serious and if he is, why don't we just take what he's offering and then get on our way?"

I shook my head. "*If* he was serious—which he is not—but if he was, that would be too akin to bounty hunting, and we're not bounty hunters."

"But we—"

"No buts. I don't even like being confused with that sort. In fact, we go out of our way to avoid those folks on account that there's a bounty out there on our own heads and getting too close and mixing is bound to backfire eventually."

"I don't see how him calling us bounty hunters mixes us with them," said Hodge.

"It does."

"Well, then it ain't much difference. We took the lizard man against his will and we're delivering him for a fee. That's at least kidnapping."

"Okay," I said. "On this job, yes, we are still handing him over for a fee, but we freed him from a situation, and he was happy to come with us, not exactly kidnapping as I see it. I gave my word we'd deliver him safe and I'm sticking to it."

"But the syndicate man said he'd let us go."

Bailer grinned. "He was lying five ways."

"How you know?" asked Hodge.

"His biometrics were spiking. He certainly hasn't forgotten about our incursion, and notice how he wasn't interested in introductions?"

"I guess," said Hodge. "So what?"

"That means he's not planning on having us around long enough to bother learning our names."

Hodge touched his fingers to his temple. "Maybe that just means he wants to let us go."

I shook my head. "He ain't letting us go."

"Nine planes," said Hodge. Then he started with the questions. "Why can't anything be straight forward? What we going to do then?"

"Relax," I said.

"How much damage can they do with a single blast from one of those void cannons?"

Again, I said, "Relax."

This time, Hodge closed his mouth.

"Are you good?"

He nodded, so I went on. "The way I read the situation, the deal is his only play. We just need to play along. We position ourselves, make it like we're going to surrender, then when we have the chance, we make a run for it. Hodge, my brother, you find Lucinda and suit yourself up. I have a plan. But if they don't go for it, we'll need to be blazing."

Hodge gave me a tooth filled grin then stepped past me to exit the bridge. "Excuse me," I heard him say then turned to find Sss'karo at the door.

I smiled at the reptoid. "Seems we weren't quite as evasive as I'd thought."

His slender tongue flicked out of his closed mouth then back. From what I've read of reptiles, he was smelling the room. He repeated the flick, then said, "I heard what you sss'aid Caw-aptain. About keeping your word."

"Don't get too sentimental. We got a job, we gotta make good."

He replied with a drop of his head to the side. Maybe he was just getting a look at me from a different angle or maybe it meant nothing at all, but I determined he was reading me for truth—which compelled me to add, "They're not going to let us leave either way. We might as well take you with us." That seemed to affect him because his head went straight again.

And it was timely, because right then the com started to purr.

I gave Anson the nod and the lieutenant came back on the screen.

He was quick to it. "Are you ready to reason?" he asked.

"Sure," I said. "But we have some conditions."

"Just take a glance out your window, we have the high ground. There will be no conditions. I already told you to name your price. Give me a number, hand over your cargo, and you can be on your way."

"You're right, you do have the upper hand, and that makes me uneasy. I mean, Sol System or not, this hidden planet might as well be a backwater. How do we know you'll let us go once we hand him over?"

"Don't wear my patience. Just give me—" The lieutenant stopped speaking. He began to twitch and blink. His face flushed with confusion. But it wasn't our discussion that seemed to be irritating him. If I'd have guessed, he was making the face of a man with a thousand voices screaming in his head.

Little did I know at that second how right I was.

While this was happening, our bridge took on an ominous indigo glow.

"What's going on?" asked Anson. "Why's he—"

"It's Sss'karo," I said softly. The Indici was standing beside me, out of sight of the lieutenant. The reptoid was still as a statue, facing forward in somewhat of a trance. But as still as his body was, the furnace fueling those blue flames where his eyes should have been burned brilliantly.

I looked to the reptoid, to the screen, then back again. I had no clue how he was managing it.

On the screen, the lieutenant continued his fight to resist, his cheeks creased deep and his nose scrunched up tight. A gurgle escaped him, then an, "Arrrrnnnoooooo!" Then his brow hardened, and his eyes took on a menacing stare. And though they were two different creatures entirely—the lieutenant and the Indici—they appeared to mirror each other.

I've been to many a battle, seen mayhem and slaughter, but what I saw happen up on that ridge was particularly heinous.

There were six Mechs spread across the long crest of that hill. The mech farthest to the right—the one I figure was piloted by the lieutenant—spun its long dual barrels toward the middle of the group. Then immediately, a pulsed torrent of red flame shot out of the cannons, obliterating the second and third mechs in the line and sending a vibrating concussion through the *Jentu*. The syndicate troopers lined up beneath the mechs—those who weren't immediately incinerated—scrambled from the flames, then they too, began to fire upon each other.

Then the mech to the far left swung its guns toward the line and let loose its artillery.

The screen went blank—and it was over.

There was a pinch in my craw, and my words were dry. "Let's not wait," I said. "Get us high."

Anson ignited the engines and the *Jentu* took lift, leaving the remnants of fire fight below.

Once we were aloft, Sss'karo's blue fire dulled to its previous glow, and with twitch of his own, he came back to life. "They will not pursssue," he said.

We said nothing.

"I'll be returning to my caw-abin," he added.

I could only nod.

As he exited the bridge, Hodge entered again, a helmet on his head and an armor plate on his chest. He was holding the rail with one hand and Lucinda in the other.

"What the nine planes happened?" he said. "Were they firing on us? How'd we get up?"

What had just happened wasn't sitting well with any of us who witnessed it, so there was nothing said.

"What?" asked Hodge, his eyes darting from face to face.

Then Bailer cleared his throat. "Hrrm," he said. "Sss'karo took care of it."

"So, we're on our way to the Martian rendezvous?"

"I gave my word," I said.

"Good thing you did too," said Anson. "I think Sss'karo was impressed."

"He was," I agreed. "But when I said I gave my word, I meant my word to Slayden, not Sss'karo. If we cross Slayden, we'll have a world of troubles coming our way."

"Based on what we witnessed," said Bailer, "we have a world of troubles coming our way regardless."

In earnest, I'll tell you that as good as it was to be planet side, it was all the better to be back in the black and on our way to the rendezvous. It was just Anson, Bailer, and myself who saw what had happened up on that ridge, and I asked them to keep it to themselves. They were happy to oblige. That in itself is something that only happens on rare occasion. Anson is always on board but, as I mentioned before, Bailer likes to test rope. As it were, none of them wanted to replay the day, so getting them not to say so much wasn't all that hard. Don't get me wrong, we're tagged a kick murder squad for a reason; if killing needs to be done, then it's done. But despite our reputation, we were once military ourselves and though it may be that neither humans nor the syndicate are at the top of our lists, not a one of us cared to see those soldiers so effortlessly massacred.

What was even more troublesome is that it didn't seem to bother Sss'karo in the least. I mean, the Indici physiology isn't partial to an exhibit of feelings per se, so his matter of fact way of destruction only served to creep me and the boys out further than we'd already been. Made me question myself as to whether we'd made the right choice keeping him on board. Thankfully, Cassidy, Rhia, and Rhoe hadn't a clue as to how it went down, and as far as Hodge, he thought we just made a clean break and escaped fire, which I surely appreciated on all parts. Not so much Cassidy and the twins, they themselves are far more pragmatic than I'm comfortable with at times. But Hodge, for a such a tough, is actually quite delicate. I mean, I can't imagine what he would do with knowing Sss'karo was able mind bend like that, and if I tried to imagine I don't suppose I'd like what I'd see.

We did have some luck, though; there was no sign of pursuit. There was no one left on that ridge to report us, and if a message had gotten out from the station, it happened after we were gone. The way I figure, it's never good for a security detail to report that they failed at their sole mission, so my guess is that they wanted to keep the heist local and resolve it themselves. Besides that, it wasn't like they could send a signal direct from a hidden planet. Any communication had to be personally delivered through the Bubble, and I'm sure who ever had that honor went in only after they'd lost contact with the mechs.

Anyway, we left free and clear without anyone on our trail, and once we cleared orbit, that entire planet simply disappeared in its shimmer, like it'd never been at all.

There was just us, back in the black, Mars-bound, with a guest. And let it be said that the squad is resilient. As it was, the shadow of the day, if there was one, didn't loom. Wasn't too long before everyone settled into a routine and things were back to as normal as they could get—well, not everything. One thing we couldn't shake was Will laid out in the infirmary. The crew took turns keeping vigil, which was about all we could do. And then there was the full hold of lizard birds to contend with. Hodge took them on as a personal project. They were quiet and peaceful like, but they smelled something awful when we brought them on, and the odor worsened by the day. Every morning, Hodge put on a space suit and took up the air hose. He pressure-washed the mess off the floor of the hold and into the airlock, pulled the atmosphere back, then mopped up the deck, all while being particularly careful of his feathered friends. It didn't eliminate the smell of the birds themselves, but we were better off less the bio-waste.

And Sss'karo, he settled in too, started mingling with the crew and having dinner with us. Rhia and Rhoe prepared the vegetables they'd gathered. Hodge took several stabs at cooking the frozen lizard bird. Turns out the Indici are vegetarian. Cassidy took a particular liking to him, answering his questions, showing him how things were done. I'm not sure if he was interested because we were syns or because, to him, we were close to being mortals, or maybe he just sensed that Cassidy was nonjudging. Of course, Cassidy has a way with everyone. You could say she was built for it. And Cassidy being friendly with the Indici led the others to ease. Rhia and Rhoe taught him to play dice, Anson talked to him about engineering. If you pushed me, I'd say that even I began to find him a little less creepy.

Things took a change about a week into flight. It was late, some had gone to quarters, and I decided to take the time to sit in the infirmary with Will. A few nights before, I'd seen Bailer in there reading aloud to Will a story from the Archive. I asked him why he was doing that, and he had told me that it was something he used to do with the infirmed soldiers—mortals and syns alike. He said if there was one thing humans and syns had in common, it was that there was a good chance their minds were still working even if their bodies weren't. Reading aloud, talking to them, any interaction helped the healing process. Fascinated by the idea, I'd loaded my digital pad with some poetry.

I'm not sure if it helped Will at all, reading the stanzas aloud, but it certainly helped me. We'd done everything we could do for him—cleaned, patched him, connected everything we had onboard that could help keep him functioning. And it wasn't that he didn't look peaceful, he did—as much as he could with all of that equipment bound to him—but there was a helplessness I held for myself, not knowing if he was living or dying or both.

I suppose I'd been reading for quite some time when Cassidy and Sss'karo appeared at the door.

"Hey Cass, Sss'karo," I said, putting the digital on my lap.

Cassidy had a calmness about her. "That's nice," she said. "I didn't know you were into the works of Drahan."

"I took a liking to him during the war. There was a sergeant I served with on the fields of Kalanthia, used to recite him late at night, made it all just a bit bearable."

"Was Will that sergeant?"

"He was. Now what can I do you for?"

It was Sss'karo who answered. "It'sss what I may be able to do for you, Caw-aptain."

"On with it," I said. "Don't make me guess."

"Sss'karo has been concerned about the crew," said Cassidy. "He's sensed we've been upset. About Will. He says he thinks he can help."

"Has he now?" I said. "I thought your particular skills didn't work on synthetics like ourselves."

"You are caw-rrect," said Sss'karo. "But anyone can sssurely notissse that your caw-rew isss out of harmony."

"I see. I didn't realize we were wearing it on our sleeves."

"Thisss isss him?" Sss'karo entered the infirmary. "Your injured medic?"

"Yes," I said.

As he approached the med bed, his thin tongue slithered in and out, smelling the room. When he reached Will, he rotated his head, the way I'd become accustomed to seeing, further analyzing our fallen comrade. "He isss an important member of your caw-rew. Yes?"

"Yeah," I said.

"More than that," said Cassidy.

I nodded. "Cass speaks true. He's part of our family, he's our friend."

"What happened to him?" he asked.

"He was shot," Cassidy said. "Then his eyes went dim." She gestured to the screens at the head of the med bed and the lines that led to electrodes pasted to Will's temples, chest, and arms. "We aren't able to get a strong reading from his neural lace. Will is our medic and–other than keep his body alive with all these machines–we're at a loss as to what we can do."

"His eyes are dim," said Sss'karo, "but they are not out. I may be able to help." His head snapped toward me. "With your permission, of courssse."

"Surely," I said. "If you think you can help, then by all means."

Sss'karo laid his blue scaled hand across Will's forehead and to my astonishment, Will's eyes opened, lit bright, then they went dim again.

Under my breath, I whispered, "Nine planes."

"He is in there," said Sss'karo.

"Apparently so."

"But hisss body hasss lossst too much telinium."

"We gave him all the telinium we had, we just didn't happen to have much on hand."

"He will not lassst much longer in thisss ssstate." He shifted is hand then, talons spread wide, placed his other above the compression wrap on Will's chest. "I'm sssurprisssed that he lasssted thisss long. Thisss body can be repaired but in doing so, there isss a high-risk your friend will die."

Upon hearing this, Cassidy took Will's hand into her own. "Is there nothing we can do?" she asked.

"Sssince the neural lassse isss intact, hisss conssscience ssshould be removed, then the body can be repaired without risssk."

"That would be great," said Cassidy. "But again, we weren't able to get a strong reading on his neural lace. Not enough for a transfer anyway."

"There isss another way," said Sss'karo. "I can transfer his caw-onscience into myssself, though there is a caw-aveat. Once inside, we would not be able to transsssfer through a lassse interfassse. He would have to ssstay in my ssshell until either hisss body isss ready, or I am in physsssical caw-ontact with another vesssel with neural lassse."

"Well," I said. "If it's the only way to save Will, you should do it."

"Should we check with the others?" asked Cassidy.

"Do you think it will change things?" I asked.

"No," she said.

"Then I say we let him do his best." I gave Sss'karo a nod, he nodded back, then placed his hand on Will again, and again Will's eyes flared bright blue, then went out.

Cassidy and I set Sss'karo up on the other med bed and connected him to Will in the way he asked. By the time we finished, there was web of cables and machines between them. Of course, when the crew roused the next morning, they took notice, and when I entered the galley, they were already gathered and waiting for me to explain.

So I did. And after sharing with them exactly what had transpired, I closed with, "That's how it is and how it's going to be."

Bailer was the first to speak. "So it's only temporary?" he asked.

"It is," said Cassidy. "As soon as Will's body is healed, Sss'karo will put him back."

"Because we do have a rendezvous to deliver that Indici, and you said yourself, Cap, if we cross Slayden, we'll have a world of troubles coming our way."

"We just need more telinium to speed up the process," said Cassidy. "Then we can turn him over."

"And I'm confident," I added, "that we can get all the telinium we need once we reach Mars."

"Telinium is a miracle drug for syns but not much use to humans," said Rhia.

"True," I said.

"Well, haven't most of the colonial syns been moved further off-world?"

"There are only a few syn mortals left on Mars," said Anson. "But a lot of syn livestock. They'll have plenty telinium in their stores to keep them healthy."

I nodded. "That's how I figure, and being we're going in as livestock traders, we should be able to get our hands on what we need without too much trouble. In the meantime, we'll all need to give blood—plasma anyway."

"Sure," said Hodge, "I'll give Will all I got, but how will that help?"

"Sss'karo says our blood contains enough telinium to keep Will's body on the mend."

"Really?" asked Hodge. "We got enough telinium coursing through our veins to help him out?" He sniffed his forearm. "Sounds off to me."

"Even the trace amounts help," said Cassidy. "It's not enough to heal him full, but enough to pull him through until we get more."

Not a one of the others looked convinced.

"I'm not going to lie," I said, "I know it sounds off. But there was a chance to save Will and I took it."

Bailer poked in again. "Cassidy," he said, "is that how you saw it?"

"I brought Sss'karo to the Captain," she said. "I believe he can help him."

"That's good enough for me," he said.

It rubbed me wrong that my word wasn't good enough, but I let it slide. Mostly 'cuz I had to tend to Hodge.

"It's not good enough for me," said Hodge. "That lizard's lying in there, his eyes wide open, wires going from his head to Will's. It's just creepy. And how does this even work without a lace interface?"

"Well," I said, "for one, Sss'karo's eyes aren't wide open. He doesn't seem to have eyelids. It is a bit creepy, but he's dormant right now, and I suppose that's helping. And as far as a lace interface, Sss'karo doesn't seem to need one. That's the entirety of him helping out. My guess is he set aside a space in his brain for Will—and they're sharing it." I shrugged. "I don't rightly understand it."

"There wouldn't be enough space," said Hodge. "Everyone knows lizards got small brains."

Bailer grinned. "Works for you, big guy."

Hodge smirked. "Captain said we ain't from lizards."

I rolled an eye at Bailer. "I'm sure his brain pan is right fitted."

"Uh huh," said Hodge. "And how do we know he's not faking it just so we don't turn him in when the time comes?"

Cassidy shook her head. "He's not."

"But how do you know?"

"I know," she said. "It's hard to explain. But you had to see what we saw."

We were about a day out from Mars–our last night in the black–and I was taking my turn with my fallen friend. We'd already been taking our turns sitting with Will, but we set up an orderly rotation to regulate the transfusions. With all of the swabbing going on, the infirmary had taken on that strong disinfectant odor of rubbing alcohol you'd expect it sometimes does. Even with the *Jentu's* air circulation, the vapors hung still in the room, coated my eyes and tongue. I had a needle in one arm and held a digital pad in the other. And I was reading Drahan again—just seemed fit for the time. Psychology is a funny thing because, even though Will's conscience was in the Indici behind me, I was reading to Will's body and to be true, I figured it didn't matter which direction I was in. I was, though, a lot more convinced about it helping than when I'd started a week before. The telinium in our blood, as trace as it was, was definitely making a difference because, according to the diagnostics, the hole in Will's chest, as gaping as it had been, was visibly pulling together. And though I know better, Will's recovery had me thinking nostalgic. It was when I read the line, '*the waves roll in, the waves roll out*', that I took pause from the poetry to let Will in. "You know," I said aloud. "I may not understand just what it is the Indici is doing, but once I explained best I could to the squad, they were all in— even Rhia and Rhoe, small as they are, are giving what plasma they can to put you on the mend. Heh, but you and me, this isn't the first time we've traded blood is it? Between blaster wounds, saber cuts and what all, I seem to remember a span we spent all of our downtime in the infirmary, a line in the vein."

You know there's a misconception that syns don't exhibit emotions. That couldn't be further from the truth. We're like humans in most every way, more than we care to admit. We're just turned up a few more notches on the dial—and that means the ability to control those emotions too. So, contrary to another myth—that syns don't cry—right at that moment, talking to my brother on the table, my eyes had gone misty.

"You know what else?" I continued. "I thought you were done. The way your eyes went out. I mean, how many times did we see eyes go dim? Potter, Welsh, Bob, Freddy—I could go on and on, a dozen syns in one day on Kalanthia. So many syn soldiers, their eyes dimmed and they never came back. Now, of course, I'm sitting here wondering if those soldiers could have been saved too. Imagine that. It's a thought that's never come to me before. There's been other thoughts about the off-world conflicts. Thoughts about syns killing syns, that we were toy soldiers for the syndicate and the bureau alike–there were those thoughts. There were the thoughts that drew us, me and you, our whole band, together. But never did I ponder that spark of life we possess was any less as potent or fragile as any human's or the fact that without that spark, we're mere bags of meat. Like the poet says, *'The waves roll in and the waves roll out'.*"

Maybe the regular loss of blood plasma was making me light headed, or maybe it was the lateness of the hour, but with those words spent, a stillness followed, washed over the room, making the subtle purr of the transfuser and the interment chirp of the med bed deafening. I inhaled deeply and resettled myself in the chair; the needle slightly pinched as I shifted.

Then I went back to the digital pad and took up reading aloud where I'd left off, *"The waves roll in, the—"*

"The wavesss roll out." Sss'karo interrupted. "Damn, Ellsss. How many timesss you going to repeat it? *The wavesss roll in, the wavesss roll out, the wavesss roll in, the wavesss roll out."*

Except is didn't sound like Sss'karo. I mean it did, and it was, but when I looked at him, he seemed different. The Indici's speech was not as slow as before and he was physically more animate than his usual stiff self. His long-clawed fingers ran up his body and across the scalp, a tactile inspection of the wires and electrodes connecting him to the machines and back to Will.

"That was a clossse one," he said. "I thought they had me there."

"They?" I asked.

"Thossse Bureau Boysss behind me. Why do I sssound so ssstrange. Iss something on my—" His slender tongue slipped out and back, causing him to shake his head in a quiver. "What wasss that?"

"Will?" I asked. "Is that you?"

"Who elssse would it be, Ells?" His tongue shot out and back again. "I don't feel quite like myssself."

ABOUT THE AUTHORS

Nathan M. Beauchamp started writing stories at nine years old and never stopped. From his first grisly tales about carnivorous catfish, mole detectives, and cyborg housecats, his interests have always delved into strange waters. Nathan works in finance so that he can support his habit of putting words together in the hope that someone will read them. His hobbies include reading, photography, arguing for sport, and pondering the eventual heat death of the universe. He has published many short stories in magazines and anthologies and holds an MFA in creative writing from Western State. He lives in Colorado with his wife and two young boys. Nathan co-created the award winning YA science fiction series **Universe Eventual** where he writes as N.J. Tanger. The series includes **Chimera**, **Helios**, and **Ceres** and the prequel **Ascension**. **Universe Eventual** is available on Amazon.

Charles Barouch's quest to never stop learning has made him a fiction author, a journalist, a teacher, and a technologist. You can find some of his other fiction writings on Amazon, Nook, and Kobo. His current journalism is in the pages of International Spectrum. You can hear him speak at Otakon and Spectrum Conferences.

And, he's been known to hang out on social media platforms if you'd like to talk.

Terry R. Hill, a Texas native, was trained with two degrees in aerospace engineering. He has worked for NASA since 1997 with a very satisfying career as an engineer and project manager spanning programs from the international space station's navigation software, to next generation space suit design, to exploration mission planning, to mitigating the health effects of space on astronauts. While supporting the manned space program has been a lifetime passion, writing of different worlds, alternate futures and the human condition has filled his spare time.

Jessica West (a.k.a. West1Jess) is currently pursuing a state of self-induced psychosis, also known as writing. In the past, she has worked for Wal-Mart, a lawyer, and a bank. Now if she could just get a couple years experience with the IRS and the NSA, world domination is in the bag.

Jess lives in Acadiana with three daughters still young enough to think she's cool and a husband who knows better but likes her anyway.

For news and updates visit west1jess.com

Daniel Arthur Smith is a USA Today bestselling author. His titles include *Spectral Shift*, *Hugh Howey Lives*, *The Cathari Treasure*, *The Somali Deception*, and a few other novels and short stories. He also curates the phenomenal short fiction series *Tales from the Canyons of the Damned* and *Frontiers of Speculative Fiction*.

He was raised in Michigan and graduated from Western Michigan University where he studied philosophy, with focus on cognitive science, meta-physics, and comparative religion. He began his career as a bartender, barista, poetry house proprietor, teacher, and then became a technologist and futurist for the Fortune 100 across the Americas and Europe.

Daniel has traveled to over 300 cities in 22 countries, residing in Los Angeles, Kalamazoo, Prague, Crete, and now writes in Manhattan where he lives with his wife and young sons.

For news and updates visit danielarthursmith.com

www.ingramcontent.com/pod-product-compliance
Lightning Source LLC
Chambersburg PA
CBHW020318150626
46552CB00022B/2938